PRAISE FOR M

3x Top 10 Romance of the Year

— ALA BOOKLIST

Tom Clancy fans open to a strong female lead will clamor for more.

— DRONE, PUBLISHERS WEEKLY

(Miranda Chase is) one of the most compelling, addicting, fascinating characters in any genre since the Monk television series.

— DRONE, ERNEST DEMPSEY

(*Drone* is) the best military thriller I've read in a very long time. Love the female characters.

— SHELDON MCARTHUR, FOUNDER OF THE MYSTERY BOOKSTORE, LA

Superb!

— DRONE, BOOKLIST, STARRED REVIEW

A fabulous soaring thriller.

— TAKE OVER AT MIDNIGHT, MIDWEST BOOK REVIEW

Meticulously researched, hard-hitting, and suspenseful.

— PURE HEAT, PUBLISHERS WEEKLY, STARRED REVIEW

The first…of (a) stellar, long-running (military) romantic suspense series.

— THE NIGHT IS MINE, BOOKLIST, THE 20 BEST ROMANTIC SUSPENSE NOVELS: MODERN MASTERPIECES

Expert technical details abound, as do realistic military missions with superb imagery that will have readers feeling as if they are right there in the midst and on the edges of their seats.

— LIGHT UP THE NIGHT, RT REVIEWS, 4 1/2 STARS

Buchman has catapulted his way to the top tier of my favorite authors.

— FRESH FICTION

M L. Buchman's ability to keep the reader right in the middle of the action is amazing.

— LONG AND SHORT REVIEWS

The only thing you'll ask yourself is, "When does the next one come out?"

— WAIT UNTIL MIDNIGHT, ROMANTIC TIMES BOOK REVIEWS, 4 STARS

I knew the books would be good, but I didn't realize how good.

— NIGHT STALKERS SERIES, KIRKUS REVIEWS

CARRYING THE HEART'S LOAD

A SPECIAL OPERATIONS MILITARY ROMANCE STORY

M. L. BUCHMAN

Previously published in *An Interpretation of Moles* anthology.

Published by Buchman Bookworks, Inc.

More by this author at: www.mlbuchman.com

Cover images:

Silhouette of soldier with rifle © kaninstudio | Depositphotos

SIGN UP FOR M. L. BUCHMAN'S NEWSLETTER TODAY

and receive:
Release News
Free Short Stories
a Free book

Do it today. Do it now.
http://free-book.mlbuchman.com

Other works by M. L. Buchman: (* - also in audio)

Thrillers

Dead Chef

Swap Out!
One Chef!
Two Chef!

Miranda Chase

*Drone**
*Thunderbolt**
*Condor**

Romantic Suspense

Delta Force

*Target Engaged**
*Heart Strike**
*Wild Justice**
*Midnight Trust**

Firehawks

MAIN FLIGHT

Pure Heat
Full Blaze
*Hot Point**
*Flash of Fire**
Wild Fire

SMOKEJUMPERS

*Wildfire at Dawn**
*Wildfire at Larch Creek**
*Wildfire on the Skagit**

The Night Stalkers

MAIN FLIGHT

The Night Is Mine
I Own the Dawn
Wait Until Dark
Take Over at Midnight
Light Up the Night
Bring On the Dusk
By Break of Day

AND THE NAVY

Christmas at Steel Beach
Christmas at Peleliu Cove

WHITE HOUSE HOLIDAY

*Daniel's Christmas**
*Frank's Independence Day**
*Peter's Christmas**
*Zachary's Christmas**
*Roy's Independence Day**
*Damien's Christmas**

5E

Target of the Heart
Target Lock on Love
Target of Mine
Target of One's Own

Shadow Force: Psi

*At the Slightest Sound**
*At the Quietest Word**

White House Protection Force

*Off the Leash**
*On Your Mark**
*In the Weeds**

Contemporary Romance

Eagle Cove

Return to Eagle Cove
Recipe for Eagle Cove
Longing for Eagle Cove
Keepsake for Eagle Cove

Henderson's Ranch

*Nathan's Big Sky**
*Big Sky, Loyal Heart**
*Big Sky Dog Whisperer**

Love Abroad

Heart of the Cotswolds: England
Path of Love: Cinque Terre, Italy

Other works by M. L. Buchman:

Contemporary Romance (cont)

Where Dreams

Where Dreams are Born
Where Dreams Reside
Where Dreams Are of Christmas
Where Dreams Unfold
Where Dreams Are Written

Science Fiction / Fantasy

Deities Anonymous

Cookbook from Hell: Reheated
Saviors 101

Single Titles

The Nara Reaction
Monk's Maze
the Me and Elsie Chronicles

Non-Fiction

Strategies for Success

Managing Your Inner Artist/Writer
*Estate Planning for Authors**
Character Voice
*Narrate and Record Your Own Audiobook**

Short Story Series by M. L. Buchman:

Romantic Suspense

Delta Force

Delta Force

Firehawks

The Firehawks Lookouts
The Firehawks Hotshots
The Firebirds

The Night Stalkers

The Night Stalkers
The Night Stalkers 5E
The Night Stalkers CSAR
The Night Stalkers Wedding Stories

US Coast Guard

US Coast Guard

White House Protection Force

White House Protection Force

Contemporary Romance

Eagle Cove

Eagle Cove

Henderson's Ranch

*Henderson's Ranch**

Where Dreams

Where Dreams

Thrillers

Dead Chef

Dead Chef

Science Fiction / Fantasy

Deities Anonymous

Deities Anonymous

Other

The Future Night Stalkers
Single Titles

ABOUT THIS STORY

Delta Force Captain "Killer Kristine" *knows how to carry the load, right down to her very bones. Yanking some scientist out of a Venezuela prison is just another burden to bear.*

But the man she rescues is no average nerd. His hard questions force her to face how long she's been carrying that load. And just what's possible if she could ever set it down.

1

"Gonna be a cakewalk, Captain Killer Kristine."

"Pretty arrogant for someone who doesn't have a clue, Mankowski." She'd be damned if she'd call him by his first name. And being the only woman in the squad, there was no way she was using Master Sergeant Connie "Girlie" Mankowski's tag. Having "Girlie" be her only other option just wasn't going down.

Command must have it in for her. Actually, Command notoriously had it in for all Delta Force operators but she seemed to draw the short end of the stick a hell of a lot—or maybe it was the electrified end.

"Hey," Mankowski protested as he rewrapped his MREs. "I'm not arrogant. I'm awesome." A Delta operator who liked to talk too much—and of course he ended up on her team.

They were both sitting on the hangar deck of the USS *Peleliu* helicopter carrier doing the standard mission prep. Last she'd heard, this ship had been decommissioned. But here it was as big as life, a secret floating base for the Night Stalkers Spec Ops helicopter guys. Too bad the air jocks couldn't do shit to help on this one except dump them five klicks off the Venezuelan coast and wish them luck.

Standard mission prep included pre-dissecting their Meals-Ready-to-Eat. With a little judicious opening and culling, they could cut down the volume-per-meal they'd have to carry in their packs by as much as fifty percent and mass by thirty percent. Wrap the retained meal packets in a strip of hundred-mile-an-hour duct tape and they were good to go. Every kilo less food equaled an additional pair of thirty-round magazines for her HK416 rifle or five seventeen-round mags for her Glock sidearm.

The mission was only supposed to be ten hours. The last one-night mission she'd been on had gone for five days, so she packed enough food for two people to last three days as a compromise.

"I've walked Syria and Afghanistan. This ain't no worse." Like he was trying to impress her.

She was so immune to that crap. Her big brother had thought she was an ideal playground, until she'd nutted him so hard that he hadn't walked right for a week. That had set the tone of her life. Uncle Juan, Steve who'd missed a whole season of high school football because she'd had to shatter his foot to back him off, three guys she'd left bloody in Brooklyn, and five she'd left dead out in the Congo.

That had been another fine command decision, Puerto Rican dark didn't pass for African black anywhere except in the two-tone colorblindness of

America—white and not. Sure as hell hadn't passed her in the Congo. This time at least they were sending her into Venezuela, so her skin would be okay, if not her accent. Of course Mankowski was a Chicago white boy —target right on his fucking face—she was so screwed.

"Besides, walking beside a hot number like Killer Kristine, nobody's going to be looking at this old boy anyway. I'm safe as can be."

Kristine wondered who was going to kill this guy first, her or the nightmare that was modern-day Venezuela.

It was a bum assignment anyway: walk into a major military base in an exceptionally paranoid country, find idiot scientist, extract him out of whatever shitstorm political hole he'd gotten himself stuck in, and make sure he comes back alive and in one piece. Command had really stressed the alive and intact part of the mission—while being equally careful to not say one word about what condition men like Girlie Mankowski had to be in upon their return. Or her for that matter. But they were hella concerned about one Dr. Ray Ewing.

You know, he's one of "those" kind of scientists, her mission briefer had said.

Yeah, and you're one of "those" kind of briefers who would be clearly happy to eat his own shit and spew it back out again.

One of "those" scientists? Absentminded, unworldly, or just an arrogant know-it-all pain-in-the-ass? She *so* couldn't wait to find out which.

"Where you from, Killer?"

"Hell."

"No really."

She stopped slit-packing MREs and looked at him until he stopped opening his and faced her.

"What?"

"Hell. Really."

2

Once she was done with organizing meals, water, and ammo, she started considering how she was supposed to extract a civilian alive. She sure wasn't going to give him a weapon; he'd be as likely to shoot himself or her rather than the bad guys. But she stuffed one in her pack just in case by some miracle of Mother Mary he *did* know which end to hold it by.

She didn't wear issued armor. Between the weight and freedom of movement issues, she typically wore no more than a Dragonskin vest—even if it wasn't official issue. It worked better and weighed a quarter of the fully-plated Improved Outer Tactical Vest with its heavy ceramic plates, it just wasn't politically correct. But then she wasn't either. This time, she'd layer up with both Dragonskin and the heavy armor of the IOTV, then she'd let the eminent Dr. Ewing wear the heavy shit on the return leg.

Over that, she pulled on her MOLLE. The Modular Lightweight Load-carrying Equipment was a fancy way to say a harness vest. Its entire surface was covered with inch-wide horizontal straps, spaced an inch apart. Every Delta operator's was unique because it was wholly configurable. The base MOLLE—pronounced Molly—carried eight magazines. Then various holders of the PALS—Pouch Attachment Ladder System—were added on to an individual's preference. The various pouches interlaced through the straps in such a way that you could probably do a helicopter hoist extraction by any of them, though it had the ring on the front for that.

A lot of operators put the med kit on the very back of their rucksack—*Not gonna need it anyway.* She kept it front and center so that she didn't have to dump her pack to access it every time she was patching up some asshole who was too injured to reach the kit on their back, or worse, had dumped their pack in order to survive an op gone bad. Flares, breaching charges, timers, hydration bladder, extra mags for her sidearm and ankle piece, satellite radio, backup radio, batteries… the list was endless of what she wanted to carry. And now she had to dump half of it so that she could carry gear for some civilian who'd probably bitch the whole way.

Girlie Mankowski only whined a little about how much of it there was, but took his share after she offered to remove his pelvis with the Benchmade Infidel blade she wore in a wrist sheath if he said another word.

"Just jokin', man," he muttered to himself.

By some mutual agreement, she didn't point out that she was a woman and he didn't mutter "bitch" aloud, even if she could hear it anyway. Oddly, that's how she'd gotten her tag, she'd threatened to kill the next bastard who called her a bitch. It was Day Two of the month-long Delta Force Operator Selection. "Killer Kristine" had sounded from a Green Beret wag…and it had stuck. As had she. The Green Beret hadn't made it to Week Two—not her doing either.

Besides, the name was far too appropriate, even if no one would ever know. She let it stick because it was God's honest truth.

Cursing herself before she even did it, she tied another MOLLE harness onto her pack along with a dozen empty utility pouches threaded into the straps. Whatever the good Dr. Ray Ewing felt he needed to take out of the country, he could damn well carry it in his own rig.

"Ready, Mankowski?"

"Gotta pee."

"You've got until I reach the helo, then we're leaving you behind."

"Sure, Killer." But then he looked at her face and hurried toward the can.

Yeah, "Bitch" versus "Killer." Everyone meant it the same way. Thank God that Delta Force favored individual capabilities over team capabilities or she'd be out on her ass. Delta operators worked in solo or pairs and only came together when they had to. SEALs, however, hated breaking into smaller teams even *when* they had to—it tended to make them snivel like sad puppy dogs.

She did take the steps from the Hangar Deck up to the flight deck slowly, so the Black Hawk was just easing off its wheels when Girlie Mankowski dove through the cargo door.

"What's wrong with you, man?" He was seriously ticked, probably about the long, wet dribble down his pantleg where he'd pulled it in before he was quite done.

She knew only too damned well what was wrong with her.

3

"Five klicks back out," Mankowski whined.

The sea had been kicking up rough and their small Zodiac boat had made hard work of reaching the coast from where the Night Stalkers had dropped them. They'd made it, but a glance at the charge on the batteries said there was no way the electric motor was getting them back to the pickup point.

"We'll find some other transport. Sink it."

Mankowski groaned, but did as she instructed. She felt battered as well, but the weather was picking up and it would an even harder ride back out. No way his doctoral eminence would make it in a rubber boat even if they had the power.

With the charges set, Mankowski aimed the tiny boat out of the inner La Guaira harbor. They'd landed near the entry of the long harbor formed by a massive two-kilometer-long breakwater that arced outward and then paralleled the Venezuelan coast, creating a narrow line of protected wharves. The autopilot held the little boat in line out into the darkness, plunging over the waves that had so inundated them on the trip in.

The Zodiac made it three hundred meters out before the charges fired. Even with night-vision goggles it was hard to see the flashes that ruptured all of the bladders and destroyed the motor as well. Already unidentifiable, in seconds it would be at the bottom of the Atlantic.

"Now what?"

Kristine surveyed the long breakwater of heavy granite stone as another wave shattered on its far side and sent spray climbing skyward. She wasn't going to complain about having a bigger boat when they ventured back to sea. Even if it was physically impossible to get any wetter after their night crossing, she could feel her gear becoming heavier by the second with water weight. Especially all of the extra kit for *himself.* No one had bothered to tell lowly Delta operators why he was so damned important.

"Go find us a boat."

"*What?*"

"This harbor has commercial, ferry, and naval piers. I can see a half-dozen boats from here. Night Stalkers will be on station in five hours to retrieve us. You have four hours to find one and pick us up right here. But don't grab it until I radio that I've got him and we're coming out." She always did better on her own anyway.

Mankowski didn't look happy, but he didn't argue.

They went their separate ways. Him scouting the two kilometers of wharves to the southeast while, moving quickly over the big stones that lined the public ferry terminal; her making her way west.

Just as planned, she ducked out of the passenger

terminal, closed for the night, and slipped through the fence into the yard for the goods shipping terminal. What the satellite photos hadn't really showed was just how few container ships were willing to deliver goods to a country that could no longer pay any of its bills. Some of the largest crude reserves in the world and they were bankrupt. Beyond bankrupt, the people were starving to death before they could die of poor health care, broken sanitation, and all the other disasters here that made Brooklyn, New York look almost habitable.

She'd planned on dodging through the container field...except there were far more open spaces than containers in the yard. That wasn't at all helpful.

While she was surveying her options, one of the country's notorious blackouts conveniently rolled through. Taking the risk, she sprinted across a long open stretch. The power and lights didn't come back on until she was out of the yard, across the street, and through the electric fence that was supposed to be protecting Naval Base Antonio Picardi. She even had time to resplice the section she'd cut so that no one would know she'd crossed through. It would also make it that much faster when she crossed back out.

Inside the base, she lay under some leaves of a *palma llanera* that the wind was beating into a frenzy loud enough that she couldn't hear herself think. The storm was really kicking some unpredicted ass, which would make for better cover and made her happier that the Zodiac was at the bottom of the Atlantic.

Straight ahead lay an Olympic-sized swimming pool with diving boards, lounge chairs, folded up and now flopped over umbrellas, and a serious-looking bar and food stand, currently well-shuttered. It was almost midnight, so that made sense.

It was a good thing that the general populace wasn't starving to death or anything. Oh, wait, they were. Just the military wasn't. No wonder the assholes were loyal—they had the only cushy jobs left in the country.

At that moment, a surprisingly cold rain slashed out of the darkness.

Yep! It was a Delta-style fun night.

4

Thankfully, the Bolivarian Navy of Venezuela felt themselves to be sacrosanct. In the midst of the storm, there were very few patrols and none with night-vision gear or much interest in anything other than getting back under cover after hurrying along their prescribed routes.

In an hour she'd worked around a dormitory, mess hall, and training center—probably could have done it in half the time with how lame the patrols were. The sheeting rain didn't let up and they were doing their duty on the hustle with their heads down.

Ultimately, Building Fourteen was right where the spy for the opposition had said it would be; not all of the military loved their corrupt, paranoid president-turned-dictator-turned-total bastard. The mole had given the CIA the tip about where to find Dr. Ewing—in the secure detention facility on the third floor.

Apparently the CIA had gotten tired of waiting for the government to finally collapse under its own weight. In her estimation that wasn't the issue. The real issue was that if the military and the SEBIN secret police finally went down hard, they sure weren't going to leave behind any prisoners to tell the tale. Either way, tonight was Ewing's lucky night.

Kristine waited for the latest patrol to sweep by. Figuring that the most secure position was close behind them, she hurried along in their wake, circling Building Fourteen. As she went, she strategically placed charges she might need to make good their escape.

The moment the patrol ducked inside, she stepped out into the courtyard and gauged the height of the building—three stories, nine to ten meters. Reaching back over her left shoulder, she snagged the lifting loop on her grappling hook and pulled it and a hank of 9mm tactical line free from its PALS pouch. With a practiced flick of her wrist, she spread the three tines out and they clicked into place.

Five fast spins and she had smooth control of the spinning grapple. With a hard upward release, it soared aloft in a high arc. The coil of tactical line slid off her palm in a neat flow. For a moment she thought a gust of wind was going to ruin her throw, but an immediate counter gust dropped it well over the roof's edge. A sharp tug gave her under a meter of slippage and then a hard set that easily took her weight.

She snapped a pair of hand jumars onto the line, walked her feet up onto the wall, and began working the ascenders. They slid upward without resistance, but not downward unless she hit the release. Two minutes later, she lay on the roof pulling up the line.

The wind, which had been blocked while she was down among the buildings, whipped hard at her. Much more and they'd be in a tropical storm. Wouldn't that be a joy.

A quick tour of the roof revealed the maintenance hatch. Locked from the inside, she snapped together a thermite torch—about the size of a three-D-cell flashlight—put on dark glasses, and cut the hinges off. Five thousand degrees of fun. There were some things she loved about Delta Force, and the cool toys factor was definitely high on the list.

She dropped into the middle of Building Fourteen's detention floor. Nightlights illuminated the corridor and a guard sleeping at the far end of it. Make that drunk and asleep because her entry letting in the storm had been far from silent. She woke him up with a strip of duct tape over his mouth, then cuffed him to his heavy chair with zip ties.

"Which cell is Dr. Ewing in?" Kristine whispered in Spanish as she pressed the tip of the torch under his chin. She'd let him see it just enough to know that it was like nothing he'd ever seen before, not that she was planning to melt open his head with it. "Grunt the number of times for his number."

The guy's eyes rolled in panic.

"Now or I'll tape over your nose too and leave you to rot."

Apparently he believed her and grunted out a six.

5

Cell Six was third on the left. Through the observation window she couldn't see shit. Flipping down her night-vision goggles, she could see that it was a much larger space than she'd anticipated. A man lay asleep on a corner cot. To the other side was a long workbench with a computer and an array of stuff that looked like a chemist's lab.

She hit the light switch—which was on her side of the door—and shoved her goggles back up.

The guy on the couch rolled over and blinked his eyes hard. The face matched the briefing and she unlocked the door.

"Who?" He grunted out in Spanish, then blinked harder as he focused on her. "You don't look like the other military. I mean aside from being female."

"I'm not. I don't fit in even among female military." She dropped her pack and peeled off the IOTV body armor. She suddenly felt thirty pounds lighter. "Put this on. We're on the move."

"To where?"

"What do you care?" Then she cursed herself. He probably did. "The US, if we don't screw this up."

"Rockin'!" Not quite the staid scientist she'd been expecting. In fact, he sounded New York. And he was somewhere around her age, another detail the briefing docs hadn't included.

As she helped him into the gear, and ignored his embarrassed grunt of surprise—civilians were so fussy—as she reached between his legs to pull through the strap connecting the butt- to the groin-protectors. "You'll need this MOLLE as well." She freed it from her pack and dumped the vest over his head.

"A vest named Molly?" Ewing switched to English.

"M.O.L.L.E. Modular Lightweight Load-carrying Equipment. The pouches are for whatever you want to take from here."

"Well, that would have a silent E, not a Y sound," he continued as he moved about the room and began stuffing various items into his pockets. It looked almost random, but he didn't strike her as a random sort of guy. Still, it was an odd selection: various sealed flasks, some baggies of assorted powders, and a very dog-eared novel. "Haven't finished it yet," as he tore off the first two-thirds before she could see what it was and stuffed the last third in a plastic bag and then into a pouch. Marks for efficiency, cross off absent-minded. "English doesn't have that sound Y for a final E. If we go back to the Spanish, you would get mol-lay, like the Mexican chocolate sauce with an extra L. Still not Molly."

"Do you want to talk pronunciation all day or can we get your ass out of here?"

He stopped and glanced around the room, looking at last at the chemist's bench. "If I never have to calculate another mole of cocaine or manufacture another mole of scopolamine (which doesn't work as a truth serum no matter what the SEBIN thinks), I'll die a happy man."

"A mole?"

"Not the small one on your right cheek—which looks good on you by the way—nor the brown furry animal, though a mole of cocaine actually weighs about three brown-furry moles, a third of a kilo. I like that as a unit of measure. A mole, not the brown-furry one but the chemical one, is a six followed by twenty-three zeroes' worth of atoms. It's not actually a weight, but rather a quantity. Because it's such a simpler atom, a mole of pure carbon-12 weighs over twenty-five times less than a mole of cocaine or about point-oh-eight of a brown-furry."

"That's a bunch of atoms," she couldn't help saying. No way was she getting into a conversation about brown-furries, their mass or otherwise. And she already knew men thought she was attractive, which was way more trouble than it was worth.

"A mole, the chemical one, is about six hundred times more atoms than there are stars in the known universe. Atoms are seriously small buggers. Why are we still standing here talking about this?"

There was something about the way he talked that kept her listening. Kristine had to physically shake herself to break the mild hypnosis.

Back out in the hall, she wasn't even halfway back to the maintenance hatch when Ewing called out. "What about all of them?" He was looking at the closed cell doors.

"There's no way I can extract them with you. If I

release them all, they'd just be recaptured or gunned down."

"If they're in their cells, they don't stand a chance at all. Give me the keys."

"We don't have time for this."

Dr. Ray Ewing drew himself up to his full height—about an inch over her own five-eight—and did his best to stare down at her haughtily. The effect was also ruined by how gaunt he was. She was a little surprised that he was still upright beneath the weight of the IOTV's armor plates and everything else he'd been through. But there was no doubting his grimly determined eyes. He'd face down the Devil herself to give his fellow prisoners a chance.

Feeling small in a way she didn't appreciate, she tossed him the keys.

He unlocked the first door, then the second.

"We don't have time for this." But he ignored her mutter.

Ewing walked up to the first prisoner to stagger out into the open. "Here are the keys. Unlock every door before you leave. Every single one, *si?*" The man glanced down the hall at the muzzled guard, then nodded fiercely before snatching away the keys and moving to the next door as fast as his feet could carry him.

"They still don't have a chance, but I feel better about it."

Kristine inspected him and liked what she saw. Liked it a lot. "Do you know how to shoot a gun?"

He shook his head no.

"Good!"

That earned her a confused laugh.

She fished out the spare she'd brought for him just in

case he did, and after a moment's debate, her ankle piece as well.

"Who here knows how to shoot?" she asked the prisoners gathering in the narrow hallway. Three came forward. She handed over her two weapons with extra magazines and sent the third person to where she'd kicked aside the guard's rifle. Then she pulled out an explosive's digital timer, without the explosive attached, and set it for three minutes. Starting it, she set her own watch to match a three-minute countdown.

"You," she reached out and grabbed the first unarmed man who came to hand. "Do not let anyone leave this floor until this counter hits zero. At that time, the guards below will think there is an attack all along the north and east side. If you wait for that, then rush out of the building to the southwest, you'll stand a chance. *Comprende?*"

"*Si, bonita señorita. Si! Si! Gracias! Cero segundos,*" he held the timer with both hands like it was precious.

6

This time, Ewing came when she dragged him down the corridor to the maintenance hatch ladder. He gasped in surprise as he crawled out the hatch into the battering rain and wind. *And here comes the whining...*

"I forgot what fresh air tastes like."

"It tastes wet."

His laugh was encouraging, but he didn't look strong enough to control his own descent. She tied the end of her grapple rope to his MOLLE vest's lifting ring and took a bight of rope about her waist before guiding him over the roof's edge.

"Don't drop me," he pleaded as he eased over the lip.

"Well," she grunted as she took his weight, "you weigh a lot more than a brown-furry. More like a mole of brown-furries, but I'll try not to."

"No, that would be roughly two to the twentieth tons and that's—" she lowered him out of sight and let the wind snatch the math right out of his mouth.

By the time he was down, she was running short on time. Kristine took a loop in between her feet and hand-over-handed her way down. On the ground, she grabbed Ewing's hand so that she could gauge his capabilities and sprinted away. In another twenty-eight seconds the Venezuelan Navy was going to have something far bigger than a mysterious rope to worry about.

They rushed out past the corner of the mess hall and the dorm. He didn't stumble often, though he tended to slide around on the muddy ground. She could also feel him lagging even after a twenty-second sprint—she'd have to account for that.

Her watch hit zero just as they ducked out of sight beneath the marginal shelter of a yellow ipê tree. She hoped the freed prisoners hadn't jumped the gun. Pulling out her remote detonator, she selected all the charges she'd set to the north and east, then hit their firing transmitters simultaneously.

The whole corner of Building Fourteen seemed to explode.

"Holy shit!" Ewing cried out.

"Quiet, unless you want a patrol coming up our asses."

"You blew up the building with those poor people still in it. What kind of person are you?" He sounded seriously pissed, but at least he was a little quieter about it.

"I'm Killer Kristine. But try looking again." She needed to be in motion, but she wouldn't mind at least one person in this screwed up world thinking well of her.

Every door and most of the windows had been shattered, but she'd only used breaching charges. A flash and hard bang; most of the energy had been directed into destroying the doors themselves.

"Here," she unclipped her night-vision googles and held them out before pointing off to the west. By the fire's light, she could see the stream of prisoners departing the building in the other direction. The patrols and guards stumbled forward to stare into the firelight to the northeast like so many pigeons. It was very tempting to unsling her rifle and start picking them off, but that would draw the kind of attention she didn't want.

"They're getting away," Ewing sounded so pleased.

"We'll see." Their chances still weren't great, but at least they were free for now. "About time we were doing some of that ourselves."

7

Clear of the Naval base, out through the bypasses she'd set in the electric fence, they were resting between a pair of containers in the shipping yard that blocked the worst of the slashing rain.

"Do you have any food?"

She should have thought of that, and dug out a pair of MREs from her pack. "Pick one."

"What's the difference?"

She shrugged. "Twenty-four so-called menus; these are two of them. Once you get rid of all the extra wrappings, heaters, and candy, they're all pretty much the same."

"Why do you get rid of the candy?" He took one and began futilely tugging at one corner.

Snapping down with her wrist, her Infidel blade dropped into her palm. Hitting the release, the anodized four-inch double-edged dagger snapped out of the front of the handle.

Ewing dropped his MRE pouches in surprise. *Civilian.*

"Candy is bad luck. Never eat it on a mission." She slit open his pouches then peeked in. "You've got the Mexican Chicken. Not a bad menu, though not great cold." She slit her own. "I've got Spaghetti in Beef Sauce if you'd prefer."

"Cold spaghetti versus cold Mexican chicken. You really live the highlife. Why 'Killer Kristine'? I haven't seen you kill a single person yet."

"I was in a good mood."

"Happen much?" He dug into his pouch with a spork and began eating fast. Most civilians weren't fans of MREs, but he ate it like it was some fancy-kind-of-place good.

"That I have to kill people or that I'm in a good mood?"

"We'll start with the former," he'd finished the chicken, fruit pack, cheddar cheese-filled pretzels, and chocolate bar (which didn't count as candy so it was safe). She slit open and handed over her untouched meal and he started in on that.

Reluctant to answer, she stared up and blinked into the spattering rain that found its way between the shipping containers. *Sure! I've killed all sorts. Psychotic ragheads at two paces and hell-bent Congolese warlords at a thousand. I've taken out narco-runners in Honduras and nacro-manufacturers in Colombia.* Civilians didn't react well to hearing about such things and she'd learned to keep them to herself. *So, you're a killer for the Army?* Rather than taking them down, she'd just say, *I'm a soldier for the same government that builds your bridges and keeps your food safe.* It never seemed to work. Safer to keep her mouth shut.

"I'll take that as a yes," Ewing said between bites of

his Chocolate Chip Toaster Pastry and Italian Bread Sticks.

She shrugged. "And?" Kristine waited for whatever weird reaction was coming her way. She wasn't real hungry and didn't bother fishing out another menu.

"Not what you'd expect from a beautiful woman. That's all. Of course, first impressions don't lie, I suppose. You looked amazingly good standing there in my door all kitted up for war. I was down here doing research for their oil fields. Then they showed up one day and I became a government slave instead."

"You mean until you got caught as a spy for the CIA?"

He inspected her carefully.

"It's the only thing that fits. I've worked enough CIA special requests to know the feel of them."

"What are you?"

"You asked that before."

"You said Killer Kristine. But that's when I asked what kind of a person you were."

"I'm Delta Force. Pleased ta meetcha."

"Brooklyn! What part?"

She'd worked hard to knock it out of her voice over the years, but it had slipped out in the old pat phrase. "Along the Gowanus."

"Which side?"

"You know the good parts? Nowhere near those."

He actually laughed. "Didn't know the Gowanus had good parts."

Ewing was right, of course. The mile-long canal in the heart of Brooklyn was still one of the most polluted stretches of water in the entire country. It was a Superfund cleanup site, except no one could figure out how to clean up three centuries of toxic sludge without digging up a whole section of Brooklyn and burying it somewhere that no one cared about, like Queens.

"It *doesn't* have any good parts," as Kristine well knew. "But we lived in the part that killed my little sister when she went swimming in it one day."

"Oh God! I'm so sorry." And Ewing simply reached a hand around her shoulder in a sideways hug.

Something cracked inside her like the lightning bolt of the growing storm that briefly revealed a flash of his concerned face.

"I was supposed to take her out for an ice cream; it was so hot. Ran into some of my friends and forgot to keep an eye on her. She got bored and went swimming. Even dove down for something shiny in the mud. The toxins took her out in under a month."

And never once since had Kristine told anyone about it. Never told a soul how her family had disavowed her. How she did her best to never use her last name unless she had to in order to avoid hurting the family—another reason to not fight back against Killer Kristine. Now, here she sat with a total stranger in a raging storm in Venezuela, spilling her guts.

How the hell had that happened?

But Ewing's arm around her shoulder felt good. Despite all the gear they both wore and all the pain snarled in her gut.

It felt good.

"I grew up on Carroll Street, just a few blocks up from the canal," he whispered barely louder than the wind shrieking by overhead. "That's how I became a chemist. Trying to figure out how to fix that canal."

"Can you?" The flash of hope hurt almost as much

as the cold memory. She'd joined the Army the day of her sister's funeral—a funeral at which not a soul had sat with her or spoken to her.

"Not yet, sorry. But I still work on it when I can. That's what I brought from the cell," he patted the pouches on his MOLLE. "Whenever I could find time, I'd work on finding a reagent that might fix some aspect of the mess without killing everyone who lives near it."

She didn't know whether to be sick that there was still nothing that could save others like her sister or feel overwhelming hope that people were still trying. "Are you a good chemist?"

"Good enough that the CIA recruited me and the Venezuelan's didn't kill me when they found out." He offered the first real hope she'd felt in a long time.

She yanked out her radio. "Gotta get your ass out of here."

8

Mankowski had answered right away. "I've got a beauty staked out. Just say go and I'll be there in ten."

"Go!" Then she'd gotten Dr. Ray Ewing on the move. She now had another reason to keep him alive, a far more important one than she'd started the night with.

Again, she took his hand to keep exact tabs on him. It felt like more than that, but…something best ignored. Together, they slipped up to the end of the container alley and surveyed the surroundings. Not a soul in sight and even though the yard lights were back on, the visibility sucked beyond about twenty meters. Good.

It took them eight of the ten minutes to scoot across the shipping yard and back to the ferry terminal where she'd left Mankowski.

"We're good here," she got Ray tucked out of sight between some big boulders and a support stanchion for the ferry dock overhead that did impressively little to block the slashing storm. "We just— Oh shit!"

"What?"

She slapped her silenced sidearm into his hands. "It's loaded. There's no safety. Just aim and pull the trigger. Try not to shoot either of us in the process." Kristine unslung her HK416, powered up the night sights, and zeroed in on the approaching patrol boat.

It should be out in the middle of the channel right now.

On a foul night like tonight, it should be tied up at the pier.

It definitely shouldn't be gliding straight toward her position at the ferry landing.

The lights in the ferry terminal above them were off for the night, but there was enough splash from the commercial yard that Kristine knew she wouldn't be invisible much longer.

Only person that she could see was standing at the helm inside the high, glassed-in bridge of the seventy-five foot long patrol boat. The boat was light blue, with PG-401 painted on either side of the bow. A Gavión-class patrol boat built in the US decades ago, with fore and aft swivel-mounted machine guns. Except there was no one manning the guns.

She zeroed in on the helmsman who was…waving.

9

"Can't believe you know how to drive this thing. I'm so totally renaming you, Connie 'Boatman' Mankowski."

"Why thanks, Killer Kristine," he grinned as he backed them away from the ferry dock. "Beats the shit out of Girlie. Never could seem to shed that one. Did some time as a yacht crew off Martha's Vineyard. Pilot gave me lessons when we were running the boat empty to fetch the owners somewhere or other."

"Maybe it's time you shed Killer, Kristine," Ray said softly from close beside her, too softly for Boatman to hear.

Boatman nosed them toward the end of the breakwater, almost invisible in the spray now breaking over it.

She could only shake her head. "I'll take rear gun until we're clear. Stay in here where it's dry, Ray. It's still dumping out there."

"Ooo, never heard the Captain call any man by his first name. Look out, buddy. She's gunning for you."

Kristine considered beating the shit out of Boatman where he stood at the wheel. Not a good choice as she'd never driven anything bigger than the sunken Zodiac. She could figure it out if she had to but it wouldn't be pretty, especially not in a storm.

The wind tore at her as she stepped out the door and hung onto the rail heading aft.

"That's a mole, too." Ray… No, Ewing…no…Ray—she sighed to herself—followed her out onto the deck.

"What is? No brown-furries. No stars with twenty-one zeroes after the one—you said there was six hundred times less stars than atoms in a mole." She slogged down the three steps to the rear recovery deck, around the launch cradled there, and stepped up to the rear gun. A .50 cal M2 Browning deck gun. Sweet! Nobody had better mess with her tonight.

"Women who know math are very sexy. You realize that?"

"Soldier doesn't equal stupid," she did her best to ignore his comment. Though it might be the first time a man had called her that while not talking about her body.

"Mole, noun," he announced in a professorial tone. "A long pier or breakwater of piled rock. Actually, you get two for one, because a mole is also the harbor protected by a mole. Like a mole squared."

"A thirty-six with forty-six zeroes after it. Or do you prefer a three-point-six with forty-seven zeroes?"

"Very sexy," he whispered just a tone above another gust of wind that slashed salt water in their faces. "A mole of moles being discussed in a mole-harbor protected by a mole-breakwater," Ray sounded very pleased. "Spoken by a smart and lovely soldier lady with a mole on her cheek, who a mole-spy tipped off to my whereabouts—and I now have a belly full of mole sauce —and she's still wearing her MOLLE harness which—"

"I think we've beat that joke to death now, even if you can figure out how to work brown-furries into that sentence." She snapped safety lines from the boat to their MOLLEs and braced herself. The first storm waves were slipping around the corner of Ray's breakwater-mole and slamming into the boat. There didn't appear to be any unwanted attention due to their departure. If anyone on shore did notice, they weren't doing anything about it that she could see. Not that anyone else was dumb enough to be out in this filthy weather.

"You know you aren't responsible for her death," Ray went suddenly serious.

Kristine could only grunt at the stab that had just bypassed all of her lifetime's defenses.

"You didn't kill your sister," he declared as if he knew what the fuck he was talking about.

"*So* did!"

"No," his voice stayed dead calm. "There's a reason that the word 'accident' occurs in the English language. Have you been blaming yourself for that for your whole life?"

The lights of the inner harbor were falling behind them as the patrol boat lifted its bow into the first big wave.

"I killed her as surely as if I held the gun to her head myself."

"Did you? Goddamn it, Kristine!" Ray yanked on the shoulder strap of her MOLLE to spin her to face him. He practically shook her by it though she was definitely the stronger one. "No wonder they call you Killer. You've been killing your own soul with that load for how long?"

"My entire life since." She could taste the tears coming down her cheeks despite the sea salt spray. She hadn't cried since…since that day.

"Get a clue woman. You made yourself a Delta Force captain. And you just saved my life and the lives of how many others pretty much single-handed. Go ahead, tell me how many women could pull that off. Oh wait, let me guess: one? Maybe two? Gotta rename you Kristine the Incredible or something."

The first big surf slammed against them. She kept them anchored with one hand on the gun. They each had a hand on the other's MOLLE and the wave's force slammed them together.

While the wave disappeared behind them and the patrol boat climbed the next big one, they didn't ease back. Instead, she pulled him the last inch closer.

Maybe Dr. Ray Ewing was right and it was time to drop that load astern.

She kissed him hard as the next big wave rolled by beneath them and lifted them up.

Yes, she definitely needed a new name. And maybe, just maybe, one was finally coming her way.

If you enjoyed this, keep reading for an excerpt from a book you're going to love.

..and a review is always welcome (it really helps)…

IF YOU ENJOYED THIS, YOU'LL LOVE THE NIGHT STALKERS 5E

TARGET OF THE HEART (EXCERPT)

Major Pete Napier hovered his MH-47G Chinook helicopter ten kilometers outside of Lhasa, Tibet and a mere two inches off the tundra. A mixed action team of Delta Force and The Activity—the slipperiest intel group on the planet—flung themselves aboard.

The additional load sent an infinitesimal shift in the cyclic control in his right hand. The hydraulics to close the rear loading ramp hummed through the entire frame of the massive helicopter. By the time his crew chief could reach forward to slap an "all secure" signal against his shoulder, they were already ten feet up and fifty out. That was enough altitude. He kept the nose down as he clawed for speed in the thin air at eleven thousand feet.

"Totally worth it," one of the D-boys announced as soon as he was on the Chinook's internal intercom.

He'd have to remember to tell that to the two Black Hawks flying guard for him...when they were in a friendly country and could risk a radio transmission.

This deep inside China—or rather Chinese-held territory as the CIA's mission-briefing spook had insisted on calling it—radios attracted attention and were only used to avoid imminent death and destruction.

"Great, now I just need to get us out of this alive."

"Do that, Pete. We'd appreciate it."

He wished to hell he had a stealth bird like the one that had gone into bin Laden's compound. But the one that had crashed during that raid had been blown up. Where there was one, there were always two, but the second had gone back into hiding as thoroughly as if it had never existed. He hadn't heard a word about it since.

The Tibetan terrain was amazing, even if all he could see of it was the monochromatic green of night vision. And blackness. The largest city in Tibet lay a mere ten kilometers away and they were flying over barren wilderness. He could crash out here and no one would know for decades unless some yak herder stumbled upon them. Or were yaks in Mongolia? He was a corn-fed, white boy from Colorado, what did he know about Tibet? Most of the countries he'd flown into on Black Ops missions he'd only seen at night anyway.

While moving very, very fast.

Like now.

The inside of his visor was painted with overlapping readouts. A pre-defined terrain map, the best that modern satellite imaging could build made the first layer. This wasn't some crappy, on-line, look-at-a-picture-of-your-house display. Someone had a pile of dung outside their goat pen? He could see it, tell you how high it was, and probably say if they were pygmy goats or full-size LaManchas by the size of their shit-pellets if he zoomed in.

On top of that were projected the forward-looking infrared camera images. The FLIR imaging gave him a real-time overlay, in case someone had put an addition onto their goat shed since the last satellite pass or parked their tractor across his intended flight path.

His nervous system was paying autonomic attention to that combined landscape. He also compensated for the thin air at altitude as he instinctively chose when to start his climb over said goat shed or his swerve around it.

It was the third layer, the tactical display that had most of his attention. At least he and the two Black Hawks flying escort on him were finally on the move.

To insert this deep into Tibet, without passing over Bhutan or Nepal, they'd had to add wingtanks on the Black Hawks' hardpoints where he'd much rather have a couple banks of Hellfire missiles. Still, they had 20 mm chain guns and the crew chiefs had miniguns which was some comfort. His twin-rotor Chinook might be the biggest helicopter that the Night Stalkers flew, but it was the cargo van of Special Operations and only had two miniguns and a machine gun of its own. Though he'd put his three crew chiefs up against the best Black Hawk shooter any day.

While the action team was busy infiltrating the capital city and gathering intelligence on the particularly brutal Chinese assistant administrator, Pete and his crews had been squatting out in the wilderness under a camouflage net designed to make his helo look like just another god-forsaken Himalayan lump of granite.

Command had determined that it was better for

the helos to wait on site through the day than risk flying out and back in. He and his crew had stood shifts on guard duty, but none of them had slept. They'd been flying together too long to have any new jokes, so they'd played a lot of cribbage. He'd long ago ruled no gambling on a mission, after a fistfight had broken out about a bluff hand that cost a Marine three hundred and forty-seven dollars. Marines hated losing to Army no matter how many times it happened. They'd had to sit on him for a long time before he calmed down.

Tonight's mission was part of an on-going campaign to discredit the Chinese "presence" in Tibet on the international stage—as if occupying the country the last sixty-plus years didn't count toward ruling, whether invited or not. As usual, there was a crucial vote coming up at the U.N.—that, as usual, the Chinese could be guaranteed to ignore. However, the ever-hopeful CIA was in a hurry to make sure that any damaging information that they could validate was disseminated as thoroughly as possible prior to the vote.

Not his concern.

His concern was, were they going to pass over some Chinese sentry post at their top speed of a hundred and ninety-six miles an hour? The sentries would then call down a couple Shenyang J-16 jet fighters that could hustle along at Mach 2—over fifteen *hundred* mph—to fry his sorry ass. He knew there was a pair of them parked at Lhasa along with some older gear that would be just as effective against his three helos.

"Don't suppose you could get a move on, Pete?"

"Eat shit, Nicolai!" He was a good man to have as a copilot. Pete knew he was holding on too tight, and

Nicolai knew that a joke was the right way to ease the moment.

He, Nicolai, and the four pilots in the two Black Hawks had a long way to go tonight and he'd never make it if he stayed so tight on the controls that he could barely maneuver. Pete eased off and felt his fingers tingle with the rush of returning blood. They dove down into gorges and followed them as long as they dared. They hugged cliff walls at every opportunity to decrease their radar profile. And they climbed.

That was the true danger—they would be up near the helos' limits when they crossed over the backbone of the Himalayas in their rush for India. The air was so rarefied that they burned fuel at a prodigious rate. Their reserve didn't allow for any extended battles while crossing the border…not for any battle at all really.

It was pitch dark outside her helicopter when Captain Danielle Delacroix stamped on the left rudder pedal while giving the big Chinook right-directed control on the cyclic. It tipped her most of the way onto her side but let her continue in a straight line. A Chinook's rotors were sixty feet across—front to back they overlapped to make the spread a hundred feet long. By cross-controlling her bird to tip it, she managed to execute a straight line between two mock pylons only thirty feet apart. They were made of thin cloth so they wouldn't down the helo if you sliced one—she was the only trainee to not have cut one yet.

At her current angle of attack, she took up less than a half-rotor of width, just twenty-four feet. That left her nearly three feet to either side, sufficient as she was moving at under a hundred knots.

The training instructor sitting beside her in the copilot's seat didn't react as she swooped through the training course at Fort Campbell, Kentucky. Only child of a single mother, she was used to providing her own feedback loops, so she didn't expect anything else. Those who expected outside validation rarely survived the SOAR induction testing, never mind the two years of training that followed.

As a loner kid, Danielle had learned that self-motivated congratulations and fun were much easier to come by than external ones. She'd spent innumerable hours deep in her mind as a pre-teen superheroine. At twenty-nine she was well on her way to becoming a real life one, though Helo-girl had never been a character she'd thought of in her youth.

External validation or not, after two years of training with the U.S. Army's 160th Special Operations Aviation Regiment she was ready for some action. At least *she* was convinced that she was. But the trainers of Fort Campbell, Kentucky had not signed off on anyone in her trainee class yet. Nor had they given any hint of when they might.

She ducked ten tons of racing Chinook under a bridge and bounced into a near vertical climb to clear the power line on the far side. Like a ride on the toboggan at Terrassee Dufferin during *Le Carnaval de Québec*, only with ten thousand horsepower at her fingertips. Using her Army signing bonus—the first money in her life that was truly hers—to attend *Le Carnaval* had been her one trip back to her birthplace since her mother took them to America when she was ten.

To even apply to SOAR required five years of prior military rotorcraft experience. She had applied after seven years because of a chance encounter—or rather what she'd thought was a chance encounter at the time.

Captain Justin Roberts had been a top Chinook pilot, the one who had convinced her to switch from her beloved Black Hawk and try out the massive twin-rotor craft. One flight and she'd been a goner, begging her commander until he gave in and let her cross over to the new platform. Justin had made the jump from the 10th Mountain Division to the 160th SOAR not long after that.

Then one night she'd been having pizza in Watertown, New York a couple miles off the 10th's base at Fort Drum.

"Danielle?" Justin had greeted her with the surprise of finding a good friend in an unexpected place. Danielle had always liked Justin—even if he was a too-tall, too-handsome cowboy and completely knew it. But "good friend" was unusual for Danielle, with anyone, and Justin came close.

"Captain Roberts," as a dry greeting over the top edge of her Suzanne Brockmann novel didn't faze him in the slightest.

"Mind if I join ya?" A question he then answered for himself by sliding into the opposite seat and taking a slice of her pizza. She been thinking of taking the leftovers back to base, but that was now an idle thought.

"Are you enjoying life in SOAR?" she did her best to appear a normal, social human, a skill she'd learned by rote. *Greeting someone you knew after a time apart? Ask a question about them.* "They treating you well?"

"Whoo-ee, you have no idea, Danielle," his voice was smooth as…well, always…so she wouldn't think about it also sounding like a pickup line. He was beautiful but didn't interest her; the outgoing ones never did.

"Tell me." *Men love to talk about themselves, so let them.*

And he did. But she'd soon forgotten about her novel and would have forgotten the pizza if he hadn't reminded her to eat.

His stories shifted from intriguing to fascinating. There was a world out there that she'd been only peripherally aware of. The Night Stalkers of the 160th SOAR weren't simply better helicopter pilots, they were the most highly-trained and best-equipped ones anywhere. Their missions were pure razor's edge and Black Op dark.

He'd left her with a hundred questions and enough interest to fill out an application to the 160th Special Operations Aviation Regiment (airborne). Being a decent guy, Justin even paid for the pizza after eating half.

The speed at which she was rushed into testing told her that her meeting with Justin hadn't been by chance and that she owed him more than half a pizza next time they met. She'd asked after him a couple of times since she'd made it past the qualification exams—and the examiners' brutal interviews that had left her questioning her sanity, never mind her ability.

"Justin Roberts is presently deployed, ma'am," was the only response she'd ever gotten.

Now that she was through training—almost, had to

be soon, didn't it?—Danielle realized that was probably less of an evasion and more likely to do with the brutal op tempo the Night Stalkers maintained. The SOAR 1st Battalion had just won the coveted Lt. General Ellis D. Parker awards for Outstanding Combat Aviation Battalion *and* Aviation Battalion of the Year. They'd been on deployment every single day of the last year, actually of the last decade-plus since 9/11.

The very first Special Forces boots on the ground in Afghanistan were delivered that October by the Night Stalkers and nothing had slacked off since. Justin might be in the 5th battalion D company, but they were just as heavily assigned as the 1st.

Part of the recruits' training had included tours in Afghanistan. But unlike their prior deployments, these were brief, intense, and then they'd be back in the States pushing to integrate their new skills.

SOAR needed her training to end and so did she.

Danielle was ready for the job, in her own, inestimable opinion. But she wasn't going to get there until the trainers signed off that she'd reached fully mission-qualified proficiency. FMQ was the gold star of the Night Stalkers pipeline.

The Fort Campbell training course was never set up the same from one flight to the next, but it always had a time limit. The time would be short and they didn't tell you what it was. So she drove the Chinook for all it was worth like Regina Jaquess waterskiing her way to U.S. Ski Team Female Athlete of the Year.

The Night Stalkers were a damned secretive lot, and after two years of training, she understood why. With seven years flying for the 10th, she'd thought she was good.

She'd been repeatedly lauded as one of the top pilots at Fort Drum.

The Night Stalkers had offered an education in what it really meant to fly. In the two years of training, she'd flown more hours than in the seven years prior, despite two deployments to Iraq. And spent more time in the classroom than her life-to-date accumulated flight hours.

But she was ready now. It was *très viscérale,* right down in her bones she could feel it. The Chinook was as much a part of her nervous system as breathing.

Too bad they didn't build men the way they built the big Chinooks—especially the MH-47G which were built specifically to SOAR's requirements. The aircraft were steady, trustworthy, and the most immensely powerful helicopters deployed in the U.S. Army—what more could a girl ask for? But finding a superhero man to go with her superhero helicopter was just a fantasy for a lonely girl who'd once had dreams of more.

She dove down into a canyon and slid to a hover mere inches over the reservoir inside the thirty-second window laid out on the flight plan.

Danielle resisted a sigh. She was ready for something to happen and to happen soon.

PETE'S CHINOOK and his two escort Black Hawks crossed into the mountainous province of Sikkim, India ten feet over the glaciers and still moving fast. It was an hour before dawn, they'd made it out of China while it was still dark.

"Thirty minutes of fuel remaining," Nicolai said it like a personal challenge when they hit the border.

"Thanks, I never would have noticed."

It had been a nail-biting tradeoff: the more fuel he burned, the more easily he climbed due to the lighter load. The more he climbed, the faster he burned what little fuel remained.

Safe in Indian airspace he climbed hard as Nicolai counted down the minutes remaining, burning fuel even faster than he had been while crossing the mountains of southern Tibet. They caught up with the U.S. Air Force HC-130P Combat King refueling tanker with only ten minutes of fuel left.

"Ram that bitch," Nicolai called out.

Pete extended the refueling probe which reached only a few feet beyond the forward edge of the rotor blade and drove at the basket trailing behind the tanker on its long hose.

He nailed it on the first try despite the fluky winds. Striking the valve in the basket with over four hundred pounds of pressure, a clamp snapped over the refueling probe and Jet A fuel shot into his tanks.

His helo had the least fuel due to having the most men aboard, so he was first in line. His Number Two picked up the second refueling basket trailing off the other wing of the Combat King. Thirty seconds and three hundred gallons later and he was breathing much more easily.

"Ah," Nicolai sighed. "It is better than the sex," his thick Russian accent only ever surfaced in this moment or in a bar while picking up women.

"Hey, Nicolai," Nicky the Greek called over the intercom from his crew chief position seated behind Pete. "Do you make love in Russian?"

A question Pete had always been careful to avoid.

"For you, I make special exception." That got a laugh over the system.

Which explained why Pete always kept his mouth shut at this moment.

"The ladies, Nicolai? What about the ladies?" Alfie the portside gunner asked.

"Ah," he sighed happily as he signaled that the other helos had finished their refueling and formed up to either side, "the ladies love the Russian. They don't need to know I grew up in Maryland and I learn my great-great-grandfather's native tongue at the University called Virginia."

He sounded so pleased that Pete wished he'd done the same rather than study Japanese and Mandarin.

Another two hours of—Thank God—straight-and-level flight at altitude through the breaking dawn and they landed on the aircraft carrier awaiting them in the Bay of Bengal. India had agreed to turn a blind eye as long as the Americans never actually touched their soil.

Once standing on the deck—and the worst of the kinks had been worked out—he pulled his team together: six pilots and seven crew chiefs.

"Honor to serve!" He saluted them sharply.

"Hell yeah!" They shouted in unison and saluted in turn. It was their version of spiking the football in the end zone.

A petty officer in a bright green vest appeared at his elbow, "Follow me please, sir." He pointed toward the Navy-gray command structure that towered above the carrier's deck. The rear admiral of the entire carrier strike group was waiting for him just outside the entrance. Not a good idea to keep a one-star waiting, so he waved at the team.

"See you in the mess for dinner," he shouted to the crew over the noise of an F-18 Hornet fighter jet trapping on the #2 wire. After two days of surviving on MREs while squatting on the Tibetan tundra, he was ready for a steak, a burger, a mountain of pasta, whatever. Or maybe all three.

The green escorted him across the hazards of the busy flight deck. Pete had kept his helmet on to buffer the noise, but even at that he winced as another Hornet fired up and was flung aloft by the catapult.

"Orders, Major Napier," the Rear Admiral handed him a folded sheet the moment he arrived. "Hate to lose you." He saluted, which Pete automatically returned before looking down at the sheet of paper in his hands. The man was gone before the import of Pete's orders slammed in.

A different green-clad deckhand showed up with Pete's duffle bag and began guiding him toward a loading C-2 Greyhound twin-prop airplane. It was parked Number Two for the launch catapult, close behind the raised jet-blast deflector.

His crew, being led across in the opposite direction to return to the berthing decks below, looked at him aghast.

"Stateside," was all he managed to gasp out as they passed.

A stream of foul cursing followed him from behind. Their crew was tight. Why the hell was Command breaking it up?

And what in the name of fuck-all had he done to deserve this?

He glanced at the orders again as he stumbled up the Greyhound's rear ramp and crash landed into a seat.

Training rookies?
It was worse than a demotion.
This was punishment.

Keep reading at fine retailers everywhere.
Target of the Heart
...and don't forget that review. It really helps me out.

ABOUT THE AUTHOR

M.L. Buchman started the first of over 60 novels, 100 short stories, and a fast-growing pile of audiobooks while flying from South Korea to ride his bicycle across the Australian Outback. Part of a solo around the world trip that ultimately launched his writing career in: thrillers, military romantic suspense, contemporary romance, and SF/F.

Recently named in *The 20 Best Romantic Suspense Novels: Modern Masterpieces* by ALA's Booklist, they have also selected his works three times as "Top-10 Romance Novel of the Year." His thrillers have been praised noting, "Tom Clancy fans will clamor for more."

As a 30-year project manager with a geophysics degree who has: designed and built houses, flown and jumped out of planes, and solo-sailed a 50' ketch, he is awed by what's possible. More at: www.mlbuchman.com.

Other works by M. L. Buchman: *(* - also in audio)*

Thrillers

Dead Chef

Swap Out!
One Chef!
Two Chef!

Miranda Chase

*Drone**
*Thunderbolt**
*Condor**

Romantic Suspense

Delta Force

*Target Engaged**
*Heart Strike**
*Wild Justice**
*Midnight Trust**

Firehawks

MAIN FLIGHT

Pure Heat
Full Blaze
*Hot Point**
*Flash of Fire**
Wild Fire

SMOKEJUMPERS

*Wildfire at Dawn**
*Wildfire at Larch Creek**
*Wildfire on the Skagit**

The Night Stalkers

MAIN FLIGHT

The Night Is Mine
I Own the Dawn
Wait Until Dark
Take Over at Midnight
Light Up the Night
Bring On the Dusk
By Break of Day

AND THE NAVY

Christmas at Steel Beach
Christmas at Peleliu Cove

WHITE HOUSE HOLIDAY

*Daniel's Christmas**
*Frank's Independence Day**
*Peter's Christmas**
*Zachary's Christmas**
*Roy's Independence Day**
*Damien's Christmas**

5E

Target of the Heart
Target Lock on Love
Target of Mine
Target of One's Own

Shadow Force: Psi

*At the Slightest Sound**
*At the Quietest Word**

White House Protection Force

*Off the Leash**
*On Your Mark**
*In the Weeds**

Contemporary Romance

Eagle Cove

Return to Eagle Cove
Recipe for Eagle Cove
Longing for Eagle Cove
Keepsake for Eagle Cove

Henderson's Ranch

*Nathan's Big Sky**
*Big Sky, Loyal Heart**
*Big Sky Dog Whisperer**

Love Abroad

Heart of the Cotswolds: England
Path of Love: Cinque Terre, Italy

Other works by M. L. Buchman:

Contemporary Romance (cont)

Where Dreams

Where Dreams are Born
Where Dreams Reside
Where Dreams Are of Christmas
Where Dreams Unfold
Where Dreams Are Written

Science Fiction / Fantasy

Deities Anonymous

Cookbook from Hell: Reheated
Saviors 101

Single Titles

The Nara Reaction
Monk's Maze
the Me and Elsie Chronicles

Non-Fiction

Strategies for Success

Managing Your Inner Artist/Writer
*Estate Planning for Authors**
Character Voice
*Narrate and Record Your Own Audiobook**

Short Story Series by M. L. Buchman:

Romantic Suspense

Delta Force

Delta Force

Firehawks

The Firehawks Lookouts
The Firehawks Hotshots
The Firebirds

The Night Stalkers

The Night Stalkers
The Night Stalkers 5E
The Night Stalkers CSAR
The Night Stalkers Wedding Stories

US Coast Guard

US Coast Guard

White House Protection Force

White House Protection Force

Contemporary Romance

Eagle Cove

Eagle Cove

Henderson's Ranch

*Henderson's Ranch**

Where Dreams

Where Dreams

Thrillers

Dead Chef

Dead Chef

Science Fiction / Fantasy

Deities Anonymous

Deities Anonymous

Other

The Future Night Stalkers
Single Titles

SIGN UP FOR M. L. BUCHMAN'S NEWSLETTER TODAY

and receive:
Release News
Free Short Stories
a Free Book

Do it today. Do it now.
http://free-book.mlbuchman.com

Printed in Great Britain
by Amazon

35907850R00040